Hero

Hero

Pete Johnson

With illustrations by
Jen Collins

Barrington Stoke

First published in 2010 in Great Britain by
Barrington Stoke Ltd
18 Walker Street, Edinburgh, EH3 7LP

www.barringtonstoke.co.uk

This edition first published 2015

A CIP catalogue record for this book is available
from the British Library upon request

ISBN: 978-1-78112-478-9

Printed in China by Leo

Contents

Chapter 1
A Missing Sister

"Oh, Luke," Mum cried, "I think Sophie's run away."

"Great," I said. "Can I have her computer?"

I'd just got home from a football match. I hadn't played well and we'd lost. So the last thing I cared about was my annoying sister, Sophie.

"Can I have her bedroom as well?" I asked.

I was older than her. But she had got the bigger bedroom. That was so unfair, but then, Sophie was very spoilt.

"Luke, this isn't funny," said Mum. "Sophie should have been home over an hour ago." Then she added, "Sophie and I had a row this morning."

I was sorry I'd missed that.

"What about?" I asked.

Mum sighed. "I had to pull her out of bed again this morning. I don't know what time she got to school. So I told her off for being lazy ..."

"Which she is," I told Mum.

"And for leaving her room in a mess," she went on.

"Sophie's always getting away with things," I said. "You were right to have a go at her."

"But now she hasn't come home," said Mum. "I've tried ringing some of her friends, but they were no help. Oh, Luke, where is she?"

"She's not that late, Mum," I said. "She'll turn up."

Then Mum said, "That girl who lives up the road – Julie. She and Sophie are friends, aren't they?"

"They were," I said. But I was sure they'd just had a big row.

"Well, Luke, I'm going to see Julie now," said Mum.

I wasn't sure that Julie knew anything. But I sensed Mum just wanted to do something.

I raided the fridge and switched on the TV.
But I couldn't concentrate. Where was Sophie?
I didn't like her much, but she was my sister.

And then my mobile rang

"Hi, Luke, it's Amy." She was Sophie's latest
best friend. But I was amazed that Amy was
ringing me. She and I never spoke.

"It's about Sophie," said Amy. Her voice
sounded really worried.

"Has something happened to her?" I asked.

"Yes," Amy wailed.

"What?" I demanded.

"Oh, Luke, you know where I live, don't you? Come round here right away." Amy was nearly crying now.

"Has Sophie been in an accident?" A shudder ran through me as I asked this.

"Just get here, please," said Amy and rang off.

My hand shook as I left Mum a note. I wrote, "GONE TO FIND SOPHIE," then raced out of the house.

Chapter 2
What Brad Said

I didn't need to ring on Amy's doorbell. She was waiting for me.

She nodded at the kitchen, from which a TV blared out. "They're in there," she said. Amy lived with her grandparents, so I guessed she meant them. "It's best if they don't know anything about this," she hissed. That seemed a bit odd.

"Sophie's upstairs in my bedroom," Amy went on. "She's very badly hurt," she added.

I gulped and followed Amy upstairs.

The bedroom was really dark. I could just make out my sister lying on top of the bed. I groped my way to her.

"What's happened to you?" I asked.

"Oh, Luke," cried Sophie. "I've been dumped."

I laughed with relief. "Oh, is that all?" I said.

"All?" cried Amy. "Do you know what your sister has been through?   No, you're a boy, how could you? Well, I'll tell you." She was shouting right in my face now. "Sophie will never get over the pain!"

Sophie nodded slowly in gloomy agreement.

"Sophie is being so brave," Amy went on.

"Is she?" I muttered. I could hardly see her.

"But she knows that Brad has messed up her life – for ever," said Amy.

"What are you talking about?" I began.

But then Amy sighed right in my face. "Why are all boys so useless? At least try and help your sister," she snapped.

I gulped. "All right," I began. Then I burst out, "But Brad's a total idiot." Yet girls think Brad is fit. He's the one they all fancy.

And my sister was so excited when Brad asked her to go out with him. But from the start he mucked her about. One time he was going to meet her in this café, only he never turned up. She came home crying and saying how she hated him. Then, at about two o'clock in the morning, Brad started chucking stones up at her window, begging her to forgive him. Of course she did. Big yawn.

"Look, just forget Brad and move on," I said.

"It's not as easy as that," said Amy. "First of all, Brad never told Sophie she was dumped. She had to find out from another girl. Can you imagine how horrible that was?"

"Oh, yeah, terrible," I said. Right now I just wanted to go home and have my tea. I was starving.

"And he's been saying things about Sophie too," said Amy.

"What sort of things?" I asked. I was really listening now.

"I don't want to repeat them," said Amy. "But I told Sophie everything that he'd said."

"Brad even said," cried Sophie, her voice shaking, "that I haven't got a proper dad."

I felt my fists clench. Dad walked out on Mum, Sophie and me about two years ago. We hardly ever see him now.

"Brad should just shut up," I said angrily. "Dad's got nothing to do with him."

Suddenly I felt a rush of anger. "You deserve better than Brad – much better. And he'd better stop saying stuff about you ... or I'll fight him."

The moment I said that everyone cheered up. Amy even switched on some lights and asked if I wanted a cup of coffee.

"And are you hungry?" asked Amy.

"My brother's always hungry," said Sophie, but she said it quite warmly. So Amy rushed down to the kitchen to get me coffee and biscuits.

And Sophie told me what she was doing here. "After all the stuff Brad said about me," she cried, "I can't face anyone ever again. So I'm going to hide up in Amy's attic. She'll bring me food and water. And I'll be fine." She gave a deep sigh.

"But you can't …" I began.

Sophie stared at me. "Luke, I'm never leaving this house. But don't worry about me up in my attic of pain. What does it matter I'll never love anyone again?" Then she added, "You can tell Mum I'm safe – but not where I'm hiding. One day in the future, Mum might be able to see me. And, Luke, can you bring me my teddy? I'd like to have something to remind me of my old life."

Sophie was talking rubbish. This didn't surprise me as my sister is totally mad. And any other time I'd just have laughed and laughed. But today I didn't. Instead I explained to Sophie quite gently why she couldn't live in Amy's attic. And here's the amazing thing – Sophie listened to me.

Then Amy came back with my coffee and a large plate of chocolate biscuits.

"Luke's changed my mind," said Sophie. "I've got to go home for Mum's sake. She'd miss me too much."

"Oh." Amy looked really amazed. But then she and Sophie hugged. "You're so brave, Sophie," cried Amy. "I'm very, very proud of you."

"It's all thanks to Luke," said Sophie.

I felt a little glow of pride. Yes, I'd sorted everything out. And for the first time I sort of liked having a sister.

Then Amy said, "And it's all arranged, Luke."

I was puzzled. "What is?"

"Your fight with Brad," she said.

"My what?" I gasped, my head nearly falling off with shock.

"You did say you'd stand up for me," cried Sophie.

"You did, Luke," said Amy.

"Well, yes ..." I began.

"I spoke to one of Brad's mates," said Amy. "And Brad will meet you in the town centre when he finishes work tomorrow. I said you wanted to punch Brad's face in. That's the sort of thing you boys say, isn't it?"

I was too shocked to answer.

"And thanks so much for doing this," said Sophie. "I can face people again because of you. You're the best brother in the whole world."

"And you can eat every one of those chocolate biscuits if you like," added Amy.

But I couldn't speak or eat.

What had I got myself into?

Chapter 3
The Fight of the Year

"You're mad," said Ray at school the next day. The news about my fight with Brad had raced round the school. Everyone was talking about it – Ray, too, and he's been my best mate since we started school.

"When was the last time you were in a fight?" asked Ray.

"Well ... er," I began.

"Exactly," said Ray. "You and I are thinkers – not fighters. And everyone says that Brad's supposed to be a really good fighter," he added.

"I do know," I said with a groan. "But thanks for telling me again."

"You'll have to hit him first," said Ray. Then he thought for a moment. "But I'm not at all sure you can do that."

Neither was I.

"You'll just have to be ill," said Ray. "Say you've gone down with measles or scarlet fever – or something."

I shook my head and whispered, "No, I can't let Sophie down."

For once, the school day rushed past. And soon Ray and I were walking out of school. Sophie and Amy were waiting for me.

"Here he is," said Sophie. "My wonderful brother."

"Oh, yuk," Ray whispered to me.

Sophie normally takes no notice of Ray. Today she gave him a big smile too and asked, "Are you coming along to help Luke?"

"Yeah. Well, I won't be doing any fighting," said Ray quickly.

Sophie linked my arm. "I've got a wonderful family," she said. "Even Mum was so nice to me last night ... really understanding. She thinks you and I are going shopping together now, Luke."

Then Ray whispered, "Just don't punch Brad too hard, will you, Luke?"

"Oh, ha ha," I muttered under my breath. "You can go home if you like."

"And miss the fight of the year?" Ray hissed back. "Not likely."

Brad works in a large shoe shop. Opposite the shop was an empty bench. The four of us sat down. We got glimpses of Brad darting about the shop, with boxes of shoes.

"What does it feel like seeing Brad?" Amy asked Sophie, keenly. "Is it really painful?"

"Oh, I'm all right," began Sophie. She sounded a bit out of breath. Then she gave a weird little laugh. "Don't worry about me."

"So brave," Amy said, softly. Then she leaned forward. "Brad's pretending not to see us. But he knows Luke is here."

"I bet he's scared out of his wits now," said Ray.

"Shut up," I muttered.

"And are your hands shaking?" asked Ray.

"No!" I shouted.

"Well, mine are ... I don't want to see my best mate beaten to a pulp. Run while there's still time, Luke."

I shook my head, and then I closed my eyes for a few moments, trying to keep calm. I opened my eyes to discover a sea of faces around me.

Half of my form was now hanging about. As well as some girls I knew from Sophie's class.

I frowned and looked round. "What are you all doing here?"

"Come to support you," said a guy in my class I'd never liked much. Then he started to chant – "Fight! Fight!"

I moved about on the bench. I was not happy.

"Not nervous, are you?" asked Sophie.

"Oh, no," I lied, but my voice sounded funny.

She gave my arm a little pat. "I couldn't have got through today without you."

Then Amy called across, "And, Luke, would you ask Brad to give Sophie all her presents back? She's spent so much money on him. Sophie's far too generous, isn't she, Luke?"

I can't say I'd ever noticed, but I nodded.

Suddenly the shoe shop door opened. Brad was leaving work a few minutes early.

"Here we go," muttered Amy. "You sort him out, Luke."

I slowly got to my feet.

"You do understand I won't be helping you," said Ray.

"Yes, yes," I muttered. I was watching Brad now. We all were.

He was standing outside the shoe shop. He undid the top two buttons of his shirt. He was smiling to himself. He seemed very relaxed. "Hey, Luke, I hear you've been looking for me," he called, all easy and relaxed, as if this was all just a laugh for him.

"That's right," I called back, my voice only shaking a bit. "I am."

"All right," he said. He strolled over to me. Then we faced each other like two cowboys in an old Western film.

While beside me the chant grew louder. "Fight! Fight! Fight!"

Chapter 4
Hero?

Brad moved closer to me. He was just so full of himself. But then he was a good fighter. He knew he could beat me.

My knees were shaking. I could hardly stand up. All around me it had suddenly gone quiet. Everyone was waiting for something to happen.

Brad was right in front of me now. I never knew he had so many spots, far more than me. This cheered me up – a little.

"You've been saying bad stuff about my sister," I said.

"No, I really haven't. That's all wrong." And he smiled a stupid, really annoying smile. He was so full of himself.

"You've got to say you're very sorry to my sister now," I shouted.

He didn't answer, just smiled again. Nothing I said bothered him.

Then I thought of my sister, and how upset she was. And he didn't care at all. Brad believed he could say anything – even about our dad.

Suddenly I had this flash of white-hot anger. It was so dazzling it blinded me for a moment. I never even saw my fist lunging through the air. But it did. And I hit Brad smack on the jaw. I could hear loud cheering. But I didn't have long to enjoy that moment. Just four seconds, before Brad's fist crashed into my stomach.

I staggered back. My breath came in heavy gasps. I nearly fell over. To my surprise Ray charged forward and stopped me tumbling to the ground. Then Sophie screamed, "Leave my brother alone, you big bully!"

She and Amy raced over to me. So did a couple of other boys in my class. Everyone was fussing about me, while Brad looked on. He was not so full of himself now.

A girl cried out, "Pick on someone your own size, Brad."

"He hit me first," Brad muttered. But no one was listening. Instead, they started a new chant – "Bully! Bully! Bully!" In the end Brad turned and walked away from everyone.

"Sophie wants back all the presents she gave to you," I yelled after him. And everyone cheered as if I'd said something amazing. Brad spun round, his eyes rolling. But he didn't say another word. Then he shuffled away.

Ray grinned. "That was incredible. You totally lost that fight – and yet everyone thinks you're a hero."

Then Amy said to me, "Well done, Luke. We'll never see Brad again."

But we did – the very next day.

Chapter 5
Brad's Return

It was the following night. And I should have been at football training. I wanted to go so badly. But, instead, I was staying home with my sister. I was keeping an eye on her. I was acting like the best brother in the world.

Mum had popped out. She never found out about the fight. But she was very pleased about how friendly Sophie and I had become. We were watching a DVD together – when the doorbell rang.

I opened the door. It was Brad. He wasn't smiling confidently tonight. Instead, he looked very nervous. He whispered, "Sorry about hitting you yesterday. Are you all right now?"

"Oh, yeah, I'm all right," I said.

Then he handed me a carrier bag. "Every present Sophie gave me is in there."

"Right," I said. "I'll see Sophie gets it."

But then Sophie was standing beside me. She looked stern as she said, "And here are your presents."

She threw at him a bag with a little ring in it, and other bits of rubbish. "I don't think anything is missing," she said.

"Just one thing," said Brad, not even looking in the bag.

"What?" she snapped.

"My heart," he said. "I left that here with you, for ever."

I nearly threw up. Talk about corny. "Just go away," I said. "And don't bother my sister again. Ever."

Brad looked at Sophie. "I've been very stupid, but I never said any of that stuff ..."

"Yes, you did," I shouted at him.

"No, I didn't. It was ..."

"Not interested," I shouted, slamming the door in his face. Then I smiled at Sophie. "He won't bother you again." I was so proud of myself. I'd sorted everything out. I really was a bit of a hero.

Then I put the DVD back on. But Sophie was upstairs. She was talking on her mobile to Amy. She was telling her about Brad turning up. She was ages.

"Come on, Sophie," I called. She stomped downstairs. Then she sat glaring at the DVD with her arms folded.

"What's the matter with you?" I asked.

"Nothing," she snapped.

"No, come on, tell me."

"Well, it's you," she said.

"Me?" I was really shocked.

"Telling Brad to leave like that. You never even gave him a chance to explain. How could you do that?"

I stared at her angrily. "Well, ring him now."

"Oh, don't be stupid," she snapped again.

"Don't call me stupid!" I shouted. "I got into a fight for you."

"And you were rubbish," she said. "And now you've ruined my whole life."

Then Mum came home. "Having a nice evening, are you?" she asked.

"No," yelled Sophie and I together. Then I raced out of the door.

"Luke, where are you going?" asked Mum.

"If I run, I'll be in time for football training," I said.

Then I looked back and shouted, "And I'm never, EVER helping my sister again!"

Our books are tested
for children and young people by
children and young people.

Thanks to everyone who consulted on
a manuscript for their time and effort in
helping us to make our books better
for our readers.

Also by *Pete Johnson* ...

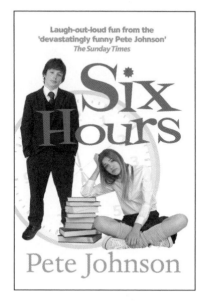

Every teenager should be allowed to take six hours off ... and just chill.

That's what Lara thinks. No wonder she is always in trouble. Dominic has never done anything wrong in his life. But Lara encourages him to escape from school with her.

Six hours of freedom stretch before them. Six hours they will never forget.

Laugh-out-loud fun from the
"devastatingly funny Pete Johnson"
The Sunday Times

Awesome

Pete Johnson

Do you look like someone famous?
Ben MacBean does.

On Ben's first day at his new school, the girls
can't keep away from him. They think he's Ben
Moore, the star of the hit show *Awesome!* There
can't be any harm in Ben playing along for a
while ... can there?

www.barringtonstoke.co.uk

*More **Gr8read** titles ...*

Klaus Vogel and the Bad Lads
DAVID ALMOND

The Bad Lads aren't really trouble. They're mischief-makers, pests and scamps. That's until Joe decides to take things a bit further.

The fire at Mr Eustance's happens the same week Klaus Vogel arrives. A scrawny kid from East Germany. A new target for Joe.

But Klaus Vogel will change things forever for the Bad Lads

Jon for Short
MALORIE BLACKMAN

As the blade flashed down in the dim light, it seemed to wink, wink, wink ...

Arms came up to ward off the flashes of light, but it did no good. The flashes got harder and faster. Harder and faster ... HARDER AND FASTER ...

Jon is in hospital. He can't move. The doctors have taken his arms and he is sure his legs are next. Will Jon ever escape?

Torrent
BERNARD ASHLEY

Tom knew better than to dive alone. But the day was so hot, and the water was so cool. He was lucky to escape with his life.

Tom's still in shock from a near-disaster in the Blue Dam when the alarm sounds in the camp site. The Dam has burst its banks, and a torrent of water is heading down the valley. Nothing that stands in its way can survive. Has Tom's luck run out?

Respect
MICHAELA MORGAN

Tully and his brother don't have much. But they do have each other. And Tully has an amazing talent. Football.

But then the First World War begins, and Tully goes on to earn respect of a different kind.

Based on the amazing true story of Walter Tull, a First World War hero.

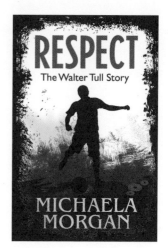

www.barringtonstoke.co.uk